KT-385-380

Where Equestria Comes To Life!

WELCOME TO EQUESTRIA

Join Twilight Sparkle and her pony friends on their amazing adventures in Equestria, where wonderful friendships make anything possible.

Princesses Celestia and Luna's royal castle is in Equestria's capital city Canterlot.

Yakyakystan is a snowy kingdom inhabited by yaks, north of the Crystal Empire.

Cutie Mark

ALL ponies are born without a Cutie Mark. These distinctive symbols appear on the ponies' sides when they discover what makes them special. Each pony's mark is unique and represents her particular talent.

The ponies live, shop and have fun in quaint Ponyville.

World of adventure

The ponies love to explore and there are lots of fabulous places in Equestria to discover.

DISTANCE NOT TO SCALE

MOUNT EVERHOOF
32,000 HOOVES

CRYSTAL EMPIRE

YAKET RANGE

FROZEN NORTH

CRYSTAL MOUNTAINS

STARLIGHTS CAVE

CLOUDSDALE

STARLIGHTS VILLAGE

TROTTINGHAM

NEIGHAGRA FALLS

MANEHATTAN

GRIFFISH ISLES

GUTO RIVER

CANTERLOT

HOLLOW SHADES

TWILIGHTS CASTLE

FOAL MOUNTAIN

FILLY DELPHIA

YONDER TO GRIFFINS

PONYVILLE

SADDLE L.

RAMBLING ROCK RIDGE

EVERFREE FOREST

RUINS

BALTIMARE

GHASTLY GORGE

BOGG

DODGE CITY

HAYSEED SWAMPS

HORSESHOE BAY

CELESTIAL SEA

ROCK FARM

APPLE LOOSA

MACINTOSH HILLS

DRAGONS BE HERE

MYSTERIOUS SOUTH

DRAGON LAIR

RIMASPI TERRITORY

Cloudsdale floats high above Equestria. It's home to the Pegasus Ponies.

Manehattan is a busy and exciting city northwest of Ponyville that the ponies love to visit.

The enchanted Everfree Forest is a mysterious place, full of wild plants and animals.

Appleloosa has acres of apple orchards and is home to some of the Earth Ponies.

Twilight Sparkle

Smart and studious Twilight Sparkle is a natural leader and kind friend. Through her love of books and learning she discovers how rewarding and powerful friendship can be.

Fact file

Cutie Mark

Race: Twilight Sparkle begins life as a Unicorn, but later transforms into an Alicorn Pony

Home: The Castle of Friendship

Talent: Magical spells

Element of Harmony: Magic

Pet: Owlowiscious

Royal pupil

Twilight Sparkle is sent to Ponyville by Princess Celestia to learn about the magic of friendship. Talented Twilight Sparkle learns wonderful magic while discovering new things about herself and her friends. Princess Celestia rewards her hard work with the title "Princess Twilight Sparkle".

Perfect prince

Shining Armor is Twilight Sparkle's BBBFF (Big Brother Best Friend Forever) and captain of the Canterlot Royal Guard. When he marries Princess Cadance, the ruler of the Crystal Empire, he becomes a royal prince, too!

8

Magical home

When she first arrives in Ponyville, Twilight Sparkle lives in the Golden Oak Library. But during a duel with evil Tirek, the library is destroyed. Her new home is the Castle of Friendship, which grows magically from the Chest of Harmony. Twilight Sparkle now lives there as the Princess of Friendship.

The Castle of Friendship

Happy helpers

Twilight Sparkle earns her Cutie Mark by magically hatching a dragon from an egg. She names the dragon Spike and they become good friends. Spike helps Twilight Sparkle with her studies and spells, along with her intelligent pet Owlowiscious.

The Golden Oak Library

MEET A LIFESIZE TWILIGHT SPARKLE!

Get set to meet Twilight Sparkle. Walk her around your room and see her lifesize!

9

PINKIE PIE

Fact file

Cutie Mark
Race: Earth Pony
Home: Sugarcube Corner
Talent: Plans parties
Element of Harmony: Laughter
Pet: Gummy

Pinkie Pie brings fun and Laughter to everything she does. She Loves planning parties and having a giggle and a gossip with her pony pals.

Party time

Whether it's a welcome, surprise or birthday party, Pinkie Pie Loves any excuse for a celebration. Pretty decorations, silly songs and yummy cakes make these super-fun occasions.

Home, sweet home

Pinkie Pie works at Sugarcube Corner, a bakery and sweetshop in Ponyville, where she helps Mr and Mrs Cake bake and sell delicious sweet treats. Above the bakery is Pinkie Pie's cosy apartment. Here she lives with her cute pet Gummy.

Family fun

Pinkie Pie grows up on a rock farm with her parents Igneous Rock Pie and Cloudy Quartz and her three sisters, Limestone, Marble and Maud Pie. It isn't much fun, so she throws a party to cheer her family up, which is how she earns her Cutie Mark.

Party pet

Pinkie Pie's pet is a cute alligator called Gummy. He loves to nibble and bite but has no teeth – so he's harmless. Gummy works with Pinkie Pie at Sugarcube Corner.

Happy hair

It's easy to tell when Pinkie Pie is happy and excited because her mane and tail fluff up, full of energy. But when Pinkie Pie feels sad her hair goes flat and she can even lose her pretty pink colour and turn grey.

Too many Pinkie Pies

When Pinkie Pie can't decide which friend to have fun with, she decides to create lots of Pinkie Pies so she doesn't miss out. But her clones soon make it impossible for her to have any fun with her friends at all!

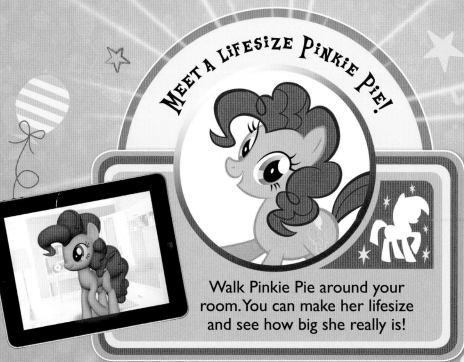

MEET A LIFESIZE PINKIE PIE!

Walk Pinkie Pie around your room. You can make her lifesize and see how big she really is!

RAINBOW DASH

Heroic and confident, Rainbow Dash loves to speed through the skies of Equestria and is always ready for adventure and fun with her pony friends.

Fact file
Cutie Mark
Race: Pegasus Pony
Home: Cloudominium, in the clouds above Ponyville
Talent: Controls the weather
Element of Harmony: Loyalty
Pet: Tank

Fast flyers

The Wonderbolts are a group of Pegasus Ponies that perform amazing flying acrobatics. Rainbow Dash dreams of joining Soarin and Spitfire's team and is thrilled when she is accepted to the Wonderbolt Academy.

Daring dash

Rainbow Dash is the first in her class to earn her Cutie Mark, when she beats some bullies in a race and creates her first Sonic Rainboom. It appears as a rainbow across the sky and begins the sequence of events that helps her friends earn their Cutie Marks, too.

Slow and steady

At first, speedy Rainbow Dash is not sure she wants a slow tortoise as a pet but Tank's bravery and loyalty finally win her over. With the help of a magic propeller and goggles, he takes to the skies and joins Rainbow Dash on her flying adventures.

Flying friends

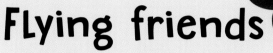

When Rainbow Dash creates a Sonic Rainboom in the Best Young Flyer competition in Cloudsdale, her pony friends are all there cheering her on!

Scootaloo

Scootaloo, the Pegasus Pony from the Cutie Mark Crusaders, idolizes Rainbow Dash. Rainbow Dash becomes a big sister figure and rescues Scootaloo when she falls from her scooter into a river after being scared by Rainbow Dash's ghost stories!

MAKE RAINBOW DASH FLY!

Make Rainbow Dash fly around your room and see her lifesize!

FLUTTERSHY

Sweet and kind Fluttershy is a gentle pony with a big heart. She is happiest when surrounded by her pony and animal friends in her cosy cottage.

Fact file

Cutie Mark
Race: Pegasus Pony
Home: Woodland Cottage
Talent: Cares for animals
Element of Harmony: Kindness
Pet: Angel

Bunny buddy

Fluttershy's pet bunny Angel is always ready to help his caring owner. He may look cute and fluffy but Angel can be very bossy, especially when he tries to make his shy friend stand up for herself.

Fearful flier

When Fluttershy first meets Twilight Sparkle she is so shy she can bearly whisper her own name! She's a reluctant flier and her timid clumsiness earns her the nickname Klutzershy. However, when she is happy she loves to sing as she flies, twirling around gracefully.

Animal appeal

Fluttershy earns her Cutie Mark when she comforts the animals who get scared by Rainbow Dash's Sonic Rainboom. She is thrilled to discover she has a special connection with animals and loves living among them on the edge of Everfree Forest.

Friendly Fluttershy

Unlike her other pony friends, Fluttershy is the only pony to believe the naughty Discord can change and use his magic for good. She shows him kindness and friendship and helps him to change his mischievous ways.

Beware the stare

Timid Fluttershy often lacks confidence, but when someone is in danger she uses her stern stare to help them out of trouble. Her powerful stare isn't something she likes to use often – only when it's needed most.

MEET FLUTTERSHY AND ANGEL!

Are you ready to meet Fluttershy and her fluffy pet Angel?

APPLEJACK

Energetic Applejack likes to gallop around Sweet Apple Acres and isn't afraid to get her hooves dirty. Her honesty and loyalty make her a trustworthy and dependable friend.

Fact file

Cutie Mark
Race: Earth Pony
Home: Sweet Apple Acres
Talent: Harvests apples
Element of Harmony: Honesty
Pet: Winona

Honest to the core

Applejack never lies but sometimes her honesty stops her from thinking about the other ponies' feelings. Her friends know she means well, though, and that they can always count on her.

Family tree

Kind Applejack is always ready to help her little sister Apple Bloom, her brother Big McIntosh and Granny Smith. Her family sometimes drive her crazy but she loves them all very much!

The big city

When Applejack is young, she leaves her family and moves to the big city Manehattan. But she gets homesick. Realizing Sweet Apple Acres is where she belongs, she returns home and gets her Cutie Mark of three apples.

Farming fun

Applejack works hard to harvest all the Sweet Apple Acres' crops, from apples and grapes to corn and carrots. She uses them to make yummy jams and cider for her pony pals.

Playful pet

Winona is Applejack's pet dog and is as hardworking and loyal as her owner. Whether she's helping with a harvest or herding stampeding cattle, Winona is always full of energy.

MEET A LIFESIZE APPLEJACK!

Get set to meet Applejack. You can make her lifesize in your own room!

Rarity

Elegant Rarity adores fashion and giving her pony pals makeovers. She teaches her friends that looking good on the outside is best when it reflects their inner beauty.

Fact file

Cutie Mark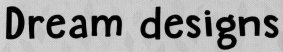

Race: Unicorn

Home: The Carousel Boutique

Talent: Designs clothes

Element of Harmony: Generosity

Pet: Opalescence

Dream designs

Rarity sells her designs at her fashion salon Carousel Boutique and dreams of one day designing for the royal Princess Celestia. She's also recently opened a shop called Canterlot Carousel!

Sparkling symbol

When Rainbow Dash's Sonic Rainboom explodes a rock to reveal sparkling gems, Rarity is inspired to use them on her costumes for the school play. Her design skills and ability to track hidden gems earn her a Cutie Mark of three blue diamonds.

Carousel Boutique

Canterlot Carousel

Pretty kitty

Opalescence often yowls and hisses at Rarity's pony customers and friends. But Rarity's pretty pet also uses her fashion sense to help out at the Carousel Boutique and reminds Rarity when there is work to be done.

Cutie beauty

Rarity talks her shy pony friend Fluttershy into modelling her fashion designs but is disappointed when Fluttershy steals her spotlight. Rarity's generous nature leads her to overcome her envy, though, and support her timid friend.

Sweet sister

Sweetie Belle is always trying to help her big sister, but her good intentions often lead to chaos. Rarity learns to be patient with her mischievous sister and the two have lots of fun together, from designing dresses to going on camping trips.

MEET A LIFESIZE RARITY!

Walk Rarity around your room. You can make her lifesize and see how big she really is!

SPIKE

Fact file

Race: Dragon
Home: The Castle of Friendship
Talent: Breathes fire

Cute and lovable Spike is a fun-loving dragon and Twilight Sparkle's best friend. Unlike the other dragons in Equestria he is kind, loyal and loves a giggle.

Royal order

Twilight Sparkle hatches Spike from a dragon egg during an entrance exam for the School for Gifted Unicorns. He helps Twilight Sparkle in her quest to learn the magic of friendship in Ponyville. He always knows when his pony friend needs help, even when she doesn't know it herself.

Spike spends most of his time with ponies but during his quest to learn about his dragon identity he meets some teenage dragons. He soon realizes that their aggressive dragon behaviour is not for him and his real home is with the ponies.

Devoted dragon

Spike has a huge crush on pretty Rarity and will do anything to impress her, including giving her a ruby gem that she longs for. His adoration brings out a softer, more sensitive side to Rarity and she grows very fond of her little dragon friend.

Dragon mail

When Spike lets out a smoky burp, his pony friends know a letter from Princess Celestia is on its way, thanks to his unique talent for sending and receiving mail by his fiery dragon breath.

Greedy guzzler

Spike loves collecting and gobbling up sparkly gems. When his greediness for gems starts to turn him into a monster, his pony pals help him to realize it's better to give than to be greedy.

MEET A LIFESIZE SPIKE!

Get ready to make friends with cute and lovable Spike!

PONY PALS

Meet some more friendly and adventurous ponies who live in Equestria, from the wise and kind Princess Celestia to sweet Baby Flurry Heart.

Princess Celestia

Princess Celestia rules Equestria from her castle in Canterlot. She makes sure there is harmony and happiness in Equestria and some say she is over a thousand moons old! Her younger sister, Princess Luna, once the bitter Nightmare Moon, rules by Celestia's side.

Princess Cadance

Princess Cadance is an Alicorn Pony and Twilight Sparkle's old foal-sitter. She's beautiful, caring and kind. A passionate protector of the Crystal Empire, she uses her magic to fend off King Sombra and rescue the Crystal Heart.

Baby Flurry Heart

Baby Flurry Heart is the baby daughter of Princess Cadance and Shining Armor. During her "Crystalling" ceremony, she accidentally shatters the Crystal Heart with her unpredictable baby Unicorn magic, creating a storm that nearly destroys the Crystal Empire. Hence she is named "Flurry Heart".

Cutie Mark Crusaders

Young Apple Bloom leads her friends Scootaloo and Sweetie Belle during their quest to get their Cutie Marks. In their long search for their talents they often end up finding trouble! They eventually earn their Cutie Marks once they realize that helping others discover their talents is more important than finding their own.

Helping hooves

When the mysterious Zecora first appears in Everfree Forest, the pony friends think she might be up to no good. They soon realize that she is a kind and a clever zebra with a useful knowledge of magical ailments.

Great granny

Granny Smith may be old but she is brave and determined. She loves to tell her grandponies Applejack, Apple Bloom and Big McIntosh tales from her past, helping them to learn as they grow. She recounts the story of how the Apple family founded Ponyville.

23

FOES AND FOILS

Equestria is a world full of friendly and caring ponies, but watch out, there are plenty of meanies to look out for too!

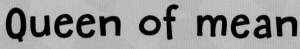

Queen of mean

Chrysalis is a scary, shape-shifting Unicorn who can make herself look like whoever she wants and loves to cause mayhem in Equestria. She tries to spoil a royal wedding and kidnaps the Cutie Mark Crusaders!

Scary ruler

King Sombra uses his dark powers to take over the Crystal Empire. Twilight Sparkle and her pony pals eventually defeat this spooky Unicorn with love, friendship and the powers of the Crystal Heart.

Lord Tirek

Lord Tirek is a centaur from Tartarus who attempts to steal magic from Equestria, but he is defeated when the Tree of Harmony chest is unlocked.

Prankster pal

Gilda the Griffon is an old friend of Rainbow Dash but when she comes to visit Ponyville she is mean to everyone. She plays tricks on Pinkie Pie and Granny Smith and bullies poor Fluttershy, finally revealing her true colours to Rainbow Dash.

Double trouble

The dishonest Flim Flam brothers are up to no good. They fool the ponies in Ponyville into buying all kinds of things, from cider to medicine, until Applejack puts a stop to their nonsense.

Foes to friends

Through kindness and friendship the pony pals help these naughty characters become nice.

Starlight Glimmer longs for a world where all ponies are equal. She will do anything to get what she wants, even stealing Cutie Marks. Twilight Sparkle helps her to see that being different is a good thing and can make friendships stronger.

The tricky Discord delights in using his powers to make mischief until Princess Celestia asks Fluttershy and her friends to reform him. Thanks to Fluttershy's caring nature, Discord slowly discovers it's also fun to use his powers for good.

Princess Luna's jealousy of her sister turns her into the evil Nightmare Moon until Twilight Sparkle helps soften her heart with the powerful Elements of Harmony. Now Luna wants to discover the joys of magic and friendship, just like Twilight Sparkle.

FRIENDSHIP ADVENTURES

The Chest of Harmony was a mystery to Twilight Sparkle, but when Lord Tirek threatens Equestria, she is determined to find the six keys to unlock it. She discovers her pony pals can help her, with the gifts they receive for teaching their virtues to others.

Generous of heart

Rarity's generous behaviour at Manehattan's Fashion Week inspires Miss Pommel, assistant to Rarity's mean fashion rival Suri, to leave and become a kinder pony. Miss Pommel thanks Rarity with some rainbow-coloured thread, which transforms into the Key of Generosity.

The Key of Generosity

Pinkie pride

When Cheese Sandwich's party plans rival her own, Pinkie Pie's pride almost ruins Rainbow Dash's party. But then Cheese Sandwich admits it is Pinkie Pie that has inspired him to become a party planner. He thanks her with the gift of his rubber chicken, Boneless, which becomes the Key of Laughter.

The Key of Laughter

Flying friends

Rainbow Dash is torn between flying with her friends and the Wonderbolts at the Equestria Games. But when her friends show their loyalty, she chooses them and helps Soarin get back onto the Wonderbolt's team. Spitfire rewards her loyalty with a golden Wonderbolt pin, which changes into the Key of Loyalty.

The Key of Loyalty

Kindness overload

Fluttershy almost spoils the Breezies migration when she pampers them too much with her kindness. She finally sends them on their way and teaches the rude Seabreeze to be kinder to his fellow Breezies. In return he gives her a flower with blue petals, which changes into the Key of Kindness.

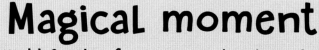

The Key of Kindness

Magical moment

Twilight Sparkle finally earns her key when she is willing to give up her magic to Lord Tirek in exchange for her friends' and Discord's safety. Discord thanks her with a medallion, which transforms into the key of magic. At last, the ponies have all six keys and can unlock the Chest of Harmony.

The Key of Magic

Honest mistake

Applejack foolishly helps Flim and Flam in their scheme with Silver Shill, to sell a worthless tonic. When she realizes the tonic is causing Granny Smith harm, she confesses her dishonesty. Shill tries to make amends too, by giving Applejack the single bit he earns, which transforms into the Key of Honesty.

The Key of Honesty

SEE THE PONY PALS TOGETHER!

In dual user mode, choose your favourite ponies and watch them interact.

FRIENDSHIP TRAIL

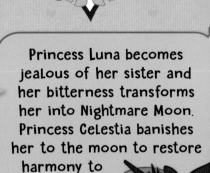

Follow the friendship trail and join the ponies and their friends on their astonishing adventures.

Princess Celestia and Luna collect the Elements of Harmony from the Tree of Harmony and use them to defeat Discord and turn him into stone.

The two royal sisters then use their magic to defeat the wicked King Sombra, turning him into a shadow and imprisoning him in the frozen north.

Princess Luna becomes jealous of her sister and her bitterness transforms her into Nightmare Moon. Princess Celestia banishes her to the moon to restore harmony to Equestria.

The pony pals discover a secret Cutie Map in the Castle of Friendship, helping them explore the magic of friendship all over Equestria.

The Castle of Friendship grows from the Chest of Harmony and Princess Celestia tells Twilight the castle is hers.

Pinkie Pie joins with Cheese Sandwich to throw Rainbow Dash the best birthday bash ever.

Twilight Sparkle completes a difficult magic spell and is transformed into an Alicorn princess.

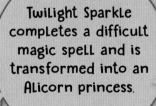

Rainbow Dash creates a Sonic Rainboom during a Cloudsdale race. The other ponies discover their talents and earn their Cutie Marks, too.

The pony pals meet each other and form a magical friendship.

Twilight and her friends find the Elements of Harmony and use them to defeat Nightmare Moon. Princess Luna returns to normal and is reunited with her sister Princess Celestia.

Rainbow Dash makes her dreams come true and enrols in the Wonderbolt Academy.

King Sombra returns in his shadow form to take control of Equestria. Princess Twilight finds the Crystal Heart and uses it to help the Crystal Ponies defeat him.

Applejack and her pet Winona save Ponyville from a herd of stampeding cows.

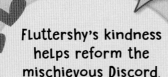

Fluttershy's kindness helps reform the mischievous Discord.

Rarity designs the beautiful dresses for Princess Cadance's royal wedding.

After the Cutie Mark Crusaders have a squabble, Discord returns, causing chaos, until the ponies use their magic to defeat and trap him in stone again.

CUSTOMIZE YOUR OWN PONIES

Now's your chance to come up with your own ponies. Choose a body, mane, tail, eyes, colour, Cutie Mark and wings. Then watch in amazement as Augmented Reality brings your unique pony designs to 3D life!

CUSTOMIZE YOUR PONY!

Step 1. Hold your device with the app open over this page.
Step 2. Tap the onscreen buttons to select your pony – its body, mane, tail, eyes, colour, Cutie Mark and wings.
Step 3. Tap the pony on the screen to rotate it and see it in amazing 3D!